STANDING in the
Mystery
Series

W9-CHL-021

MULTICULTURAL READERS SET 2

SHADOW ON THE SNOW

ANNE SCHRAFF

Artesian Press

P.O. Box 355 Buena Park, CA 90621

Project Editor: Carol E. Newell
Cover Illustrator: Fujiko
Cover Design: Tony Amaro
©2000 Artesian Press

ISBN 1-58659-088-X

Chapter 1

Huong Ngo ate lunch alone since school began. He was the only Vietnamese boy in the freshman class at the small high school. He was a little timid. Now Huong looked up from his microscope in biology class to see another boy grinning at him.

"Can you see the amoeba, man?" the boy asked.

"Yes, I can," Huong said.

"I can, too. I can finally see them! Oh, I'm Darnell Rollins. Who're you?"

"Huong Ngo," Huong said. He decided he'd take a chance and ask Darnell if he'd like to eat lunch with him. Darnell had a warm, friendly face. "Perhaps we can eat lunch together today?"

"Sure," Darnell said. "We can eat up on the hill. You can see everything from there."

At lunchtime, Huong followed Darnell up a small hill behind the school, and they sat down to eat. "We can see all the hills from here," Darnell said, "and even the wild man's cabin."

Huong's eyes widened. "The wild man?" he asked.

"Yeah, he's the guy who lives on top of Crow's Peak, and he's got long, gray hair. He yells and screams and jumps up and down when people get too close. He hates planes and cars, and I guess people, too," Darnell said.

"I wouldn't want to go near such a man," Huong said with a shudder.

"Nobody wants to," Darnell said. "When we go on field trips we stay away from Crow's Peak. Nobody knows if the guy is dangerous or not, but who wants to find out?"

Huong finished his rice and vegetables, and Darnell wolfed down the last of his ham and cheese sandwich. "You're a good guy, Darnell. I feel comfortable with you. It's hard for me to feel at ease with new people," Huong said.

"You're okay, too, Huong," Darnell replied. "Lots of guys make stupid cracks about my scars, but you didn't."

Huong had noticed the pink scars across Darnell's cheeks, but they didn't seem important. Darnell was still a big, good looking guy.

"When I was a little kid I was in a fire. A stove fell over on me. We were camping. For a long time I felt like coming to school with a burlap sack over my head. I hated it when kids teased me and gave me nicknames from monsters in horror movies. I got over that. Now I figure if guys don't like my scars, that's their problem, not mine, right?" Darnell said.

"Everybody has something somebody doesn't like," Huong said. "Like me. I'm the shortest boy in the freshman class. My first day here, a guy yells 'Hey, you better go back to junior high!'"

"Are you good in science, Huong?" Darnell asked.

"Yes, that's my favorite subject."

"Mine, too. And Mr. Levine takes us on these great field trips. We get to miss a lot of other classes and go tramping through the hills," Darnell said.

The next day, Mr. Levine assigned a field trip. "We had better get to see nature closing down for the winter before the snow flies," Mr. Levine said. "We'll assemble here at 8:00 A.M. and start out. You've all got instructions on what to bring and how to dress."

Huong read the instruction paper carefully. Good, comfortable shoes, a backpack with some healthy snacks, and a water bottle, plus a notebook and some pens or pencils.

"My first science field trip," Huong said aloud. The thought of exploring the hills delighted him. It would be even better now that he had a friend in Darnell.

At eight the next morning Huong was so eager to go on the field trip that he was the first to arrive. Minutes later a boy named Josh and a girl named Shelly came.

"Hey," Josh said to Huong, "do you eat dogs?"

"No," Huong said angrily. His cheeks turned warm.

Shelly covered her mouth with her hands and giggled. Huong felt terrible. He wished Darnell would arrive quickly.

Chapter 2

"Why are you dressed so funny?" Shelly asked Huong.

Huong heard Mr. Levine suggest students wear "grungy" clothing. Huong didn't know what that word meant. He couldn't even find it in the dictionary. Then Darnell told him it meant old, comfortable clothing that you didn't care what happened to.

"Like I'm wearing old jeans and one of Dad's old jackets with paint stains on it," Darnell explained.

So Huong borrowed his father's old windbreaker—the coat he wore when he fished for shrimp in Louisiana when the family first came to America.

"You smell like fish," Josh said.

Shelly giggled again. "He always smells like fish!"

Huong's face turned warmer still. It was true that he ate a lot of fish, rice, and vegetables, but surely he didn't smell like fish!

Suddenly Huong remembered what Darnell had said about his scar, "If guys don't like my scars, that's their problem, not mine." Huong decided he would take that attitude. He would ignore the stupid remarks.

Darnell came along then and the rest of the class quickly assembled. They fell in line behind Mr. Levine who wore oversized shoes and the worst looking old jeans Huong ever saw.

"This is going to be a dangerous hike," Josh told Huong.

"Yeah, right," Darnell said. "We might be attacked by ground squirrels. They're real testy this time of year when they're stocking up on acorns."

Huong laughed at his friend's joke.

But Josh looked offended. "No, really. We'll be hiking too close to the wild man's place. You know about the wild man, don't you, Huong?"

"I've heard of the angry man who lives alone on Crow's Peak," Huong said.

"We think he escaped from somewhere where they keep guys like him. A guy I know saw him close, and he's got real long fingernails like claws, and he screeches and howls. I hope I'm not scaring you, Huong," Josh said.

"Oh, no," Huong said. "I'm not scared. It's an interesting legend. We have legends in our culture, too."

"It's not a legend. It's true. The wild man is real, and I've heard he really hates people from Asia, Huong, your kind, you know," Josh said.

"Especially when they smell like fish," Shelly laughed.

"Maybe you smell worse than fish," Darnell said.

Shelly's eyes flashed. "I do not! How dare you say I smell bad, Darnell!"

Darnell laughed and nudged Huong. "She buys perfume by the gallon and splashes around in it. It's really stinky perfume. It's called scent of skunk."

"You can laugh all you want," Josh said, "but the wild man could be hiding in any tree along here. He could jump right out of the brush and grab you."

Darnell rolled his eyes and Huong smiled. Huong thought it was wonderful to have such a wilderness so close to school. Josh and Shelly raved on about the leeches in the creeks and the poison ivy everywhere, but Huong just ignored them. They were trying to scare him. It was fun to scare someone who was new in town. Perhaps, Huong thought, Josh and Shelly believed he was stupid enough to be frightened.

"We got special leeches," Josh said, walking alongside Huong now. "Maybe your leeches back home weren't like this. Anyway, you can be walking along, minding your own business and the leeches come flying out of a shrub or something and cling to your face. And they suck out your blood. And they just hang on until all your blood is gone, you know?"

"Like vampires," Shelly said, shaking with glee.

Chapter 3

"Oh, I think leeches are the same all over the world," Huong said very seriously. "They are worms that swim in the water or creep on land. But they never fly. They sometimes attach themselves to your legs when you swim in the river, but they don't fly from the bushes."

"You think you know more than us?" Josh demanded. "You've been in school a coupla weeks, and you think you know more than us? I'm telling you—leeches fly!"

"Leeches fly when pigs fly," Huong said.

"Well, if you're going to be like that, then we won't try to teach you anything," Josh said. "You can just learn the hard way."

They stopped on a small rise and looked down at Canyon Valley High School with its cluster of one story, sand colored buildings.

"Brrr, it's cold," Shelly complained. "That wind!"

Mr. Levine gave the girl a sour look. "I advised you to wear warm clothing. Now there you are, Shelly, in a silly little fluff of a sweater," he said.

"He is so boring!" Shelly whispered to Josh as Mr. Levine began to lecture about how autumn changed the colors of the valley.

"All teachers are boring," Josh said. "They don't hire you as a teacher unless you're a boring person."

As they climbed a hill you could see Crow's Peak and the wild man's shack.

"Do you see the wild man?" Josh asked.

"I think he's out front hitting the

ground with a shovel," Shelly laughed.

"Stop that nonsense," Mr. Levine said. "I'm tired of all the fanciful tales you people make up about a poor man who minds his own business and respects the environment."

"Look, Mr. Levine," Darnell said, "is that a cave over there?"

"Where?" Mr. Levine asked, squinting in the sunlight.

"Right over there to the north," Darnell said. "I see an entrance to a cave, I think. Come on, let's take a closer look."

They all drew close to the cave. "Lots of brush almost conceals the entrance," Mr. Levine said. "Mmmm, could be interesting to explore, but not today. I have plans for us to see the river and the crystallized rocks—if we're to be back at school by noon we must move along."

"Awww, Mr. Levine, the heck with the river and the rocks. Let's explore the cave. Maybe there's a treasure chest hidden in there or something," Josh said.

"Hardly," Mr. Levine said. "No, we'll leave the cave to another time when we are studying limestone and cavern formations. Let's march south now, towards the river. We'll have an excellent view from there of how the river has carved a path for itself through the mountains. I want you to see how approaching winter affects life in the river."

They were nearing the river when suddenly a man with a shotgun appeared in their path.

"It's the wild man!" cried Shelly.

Huong stared at the man with astonishment. He wore a wide-brimmed cowboy hat, and his long, gray hair streamed down his shoulders like smoke. His face was craggy and sunburned, and his eyes burned with inner fires.

"What do you people want?" the man demanded.

"We're taking a science field trip, sir," Mr. Levine explained, a nervous smile twitching on his lips. "No need for alarm, my friend."

"You are not my friend," the wild man snapped. "No more than any of you are friends to this ravaged land. You are all my enemies and the enemies of the wilderness!"

Chapter 4

"Wow," Shelly gasped, "now we're in for it!"

"Let's get outta here," Josh muttered.

The man gripped his shotgun and came closer. "I've been watching you. You're nothing but vandals! Despoilers of nature," he cried.

"My dear sir," Mr. Levine said, "I teach my students great respect for the land. I dare say we love and respect this beautiful wilderness as much as you do."

The long-haired man laughed savagely. "Then why are you throwing aluminium cans with jagged tops into the meadow for the poor beasts to become trapped in?" he said.

"Never!" Mr. Levine declared.

"That one ..." the wild man pointed at Josh, "he threw his can right there a moment ago."

"Nah, I didn't," Josh said in a shaky voice. He'd gulped his ginger ale and flipped the can in tall grass. What difference did one little old can like that make?

"Lying vandal," the man shouted. "Now you get that can you threw over there this minute!"

Frightened, Josh ran to retrieve the can.

"Give it to me," the man demanded.

"Sure, yeah," Josh said, tossing him the can.

The man held the can aloft. "Look at the opening. A poor beast reaching for the sweetness inside this can could get a paw trapped. In panic, trying to free itself, it could become injured. And why? *Why?* Because a vile delinquent was too lazy to carry out his own dirt!"

"I am deeply sorry, sir," Mr. Levine said. "I share your anger at this incident."

"And you," the man shouted at Shelly, "you saw a covey of quail. You deliberately hurled a rock into their midst!"

"I did not!" Shelly gasped, backing up.

"I saw you with my binoculars," the man shrieked.

"We'd better leave at once and return to the school," Mr. Levine said hurriedly.

"Go!" the man almost screamed. "Go and take your gang of vandals with you. And don't come back. This land doesn't belong to you. It belongs to the Spirit that created it and to the animals who live here without harming it. If a pack of raccoons come into your dirty town and try to enter your homes, you trap them and destroy them. What gives you the right to violate the homes of the raccoons and other animals?"

"Man, he's really nuts," Josh whispered as they scurried down the hill.

"Why did you throw the can in the grass?" Huong asked. "Mr. Levine gave us trash bags for that."

"Yeah, jerk, why did you do that?" Darnell said.

"The man probably wouldn't have bothered us if he hadn't seen such outrages," Mr. Levine fumed.

"He's a menace!" Shelly cried. "He belongs in a cage!"

"Yeah," Josh said, "where does he get the right to order us off public land? We're American citizens. Our folks pay taxes."

"We better tell the police on him," Shelly said.

"My dad's a councilman," Josh said, "and he's got clout. We'll fix that wild man's wagon for almost killing us."

"He didn't almost kill us," Huong

said.

"Yeah, he just yelled at us," Darnell said.

"He pointed his shotgun at me and said 'I'll blow you away.'," Josh said.

"That's a lie," Huong said.

"Look, fish-face," Josh yelled, "I say that's what he said, and you better not say otherwise."

"Yeah," Shelly agreed, "I heard him say 'I'll blow your head off, you little punk'."

"He didn't say that," Huong said.

"Look, we're Americans. Our parents pay taxes," Josh snarled.

"I am also an American," Huong said, "and my parents pay many taxes."

"He threatened us, and if you say otherwise, you're in trouble, Huong," Josh said in a low, angry voice.

Chapter 5

When the class returned to school, Mr. Levine told the principal what happened. She called the sheriff, who came in to talk to Mr. Levine and his class.

"The fellow was very angry, and he held a shotgun. I never saw him aim it at anyone, and he certainly didn't fire it," Mr. Levine said.

The sheriff looked out at the students. "Did he threaten any one of you directly?"

Josh raised his hand. "Yeah, he pointed the shotgun right at my head. It was about six inches from my head. He said he was gonna blow me away."

Shelly raised her hand. "He called Josh a punk, and he said the world would be better off if people like him were shot," she said.

Huong raised his hand. Josh nudged him and whispered, "You better not!" But Huong said, "Sheriff, I was looking right at the man the whole time, and he never aimed the gun at Josh. He never said those things."

Darnell raised his hand. "Yeah, he yelled at Josh for throwing a pop can in the grass, and he yelled at Shelly for throwing rocks at the quail, but he never pointed the gun at anybody. He never made those threats."

A boy named Chet nodded. "Huong and Darnell are right. The guy was yelling about the animals and stuff, but he didn't point the gun or threaten Josh."

The Sheriff asked for a show of hands. "Did anybody hear him threaten Josh and Shelly?"

All hands went up to back Huong's story.

"Josh is fibbing," a girl said, "'cause

he got mad that he was caught throwing trash in the wilderness."

"Well, what I'll do is go talk to this fellow. His name is Steven Lattimore. That's who my people call the wild man. I'll tell him he's got no business ordering people out of the wilderness. It's a National Forest," the sheriff said. "But, at the same time, anyone caught littering, and that means tossing a pop can or whatever, will be subject to a steep fine. Your teacher may want to stress that point."

Mr. Levine nodded. "Thank you, Sheriff. The field trips are very important to the learning experience in science. I was mortified that a student of mine violated a cardinal rule of not discarding trash. And that student shall receive an F for the field trip."

When the class was filing out, Josh moved alongside Huong. "I'll get you, rat fink," he hissed. Huong didn't turn. He pretended he didn't hear the boy's threat.

Josh joined a group of boys outside. "My Dad will take care of old Lattimore. You'll see," Josh boasted. "That weirdo will be off the mountain and in a cage where he belongs pretty quick."

"I think you belong in a cage, Josh," Darnell said. "What if everybody tossed a can in the woods? What do you think it'd look like? The city dump, that's what."

"Mind your own business, scarface," Josh yelled. "No wonder you like that wild man. You're a monster, too!"

When Josh's father put pressure on, Steven Lattimore was served with a restraining order stopping him from harassing any and all visitors to the forest. He faced arrest if anybody complained of harassment from him.

"Now we can go into the wilderness anytime we want and have fun," Josh said. "If we want to throw stuff, he can't do a thing."

Mr. Levine heard the remark. He came up behind Josh and said sharply, "Young man, you litter and your parents will be paying a hefty fine. I'm sure that won't make you very popular in your house!"

After school, Huong saw Josh and his friend Mick behind the library building.

"It'll drive that weirdo Lattimore crazy, and he can't do a thing!" Josh was laughing.

"But are you sure we won't get caught?" Mick asked.

Chapter 6

Huong crouched in the shadows between the library and the science building and listened.

"I'll fill a big garbage bag from one of the school trash barrels, and we'll haul it to the edge of Lattimore's cabin. Right where he can see it," Josh said.

"What a yuk!" Mick laughed. "And if I help you with this, you promise to do my Algebra homework every day for a month?"

"You bet," Josh said.

Huong rushed over to the soccer field where Darnell was finishing practice. He told Darnell everything. Both boys went to see Mr. Levine. The teacher scowled and said, "If this is true, we'll catch them red-handed. I'll take my instant camera so we have pictures on the spot."

Mr. Levine, Huong, and Darnell watched as Josh and Mick filled a garbage bag with school trash. They all followed as the two boys took turns dragging the heavy load up the hill towards Crow's Peak.

"I wish we had a camera," Josh said, "so we could take a picture of the wild man freaking out when he sees this mountain of trash!"

Darnell nudged Huong and whispered, "We do have a camera, you bozo. It won't be Lattimore freaking out!" Mr. Levine held the camera, and the flash bulb popped as Josh and Mick began unloading the contents of the garbage bag. "Hold it right there, boys," Mr. Levine shouted.

Josh turned an ashen face to the teacher. "We were, uh, cleaning up stuff we found laying around and putting it in this bag," he muttered.

"Yeah, we gathered all this trash from around here," Mick said.

Steven Lattimore charged out of his cabin, but when he saw the teacher he stopped to listen to what was going on.

"Josh, Mick, we followed you from school. We saw you fill the bag with school trash and drag it up here and begin dumping it," Mr. Levine said. "Don't make matters worse by a pathetic lie. Now clean up the trash that you spilled out, return it to the bag, and we shall go back to school."

Huong looked at Mr. Lattimore and said, "Don't you worry. We love this beautiful place, too. We will protect it."

Josh and Mick were assigned detention for a month and a half. During the extra hour they spent at school each day they would clean up trash, scrape gum off desks, and do whatever chores the janitor needed help with.

As Huong and Darnell talked about

their Saturday plans to explore the cave they'd seen on the field trip, Josh came along. "I'll get you guys for what you did," he snarled, "and don't you forget it!"

Darnell laughed. "Oh, go soak your head in a rain barrel," he said.

Huong looked forward to exploring the cave with Darnell, but when Saturday came, the sky was filled with clouds. Huong hoped the snow stayed away until they had finished exploring the cave and returned home.

Huong dressed quickly and told his parents he was doing extra credit work for science. He did think he and Darnell could complete the science special project with notes from their trip through the cave.

Huong biked down to school where Darnell waited. Josh and Mick had been given a few hours of Saturday detention, and they were already emptying trash, glaring at Huong and Darnell with hatred.

"I brought a flash camera so we can take pictures inside the cave for our reports," Darnell said.

"I brought a flashlight and plenty of notebook paper," Huong said with a grin, eager for the adventure to begin.

When the boys reached the mouth of the cave they gently cleared away the brush. A huge boulder rested above the entrance. They didn't want to disturb that.

"That big rock could squash us," Darnell said.

Chapter 7

Huong entered the cave slowly. Perhaps this cave would be large and interesting like the Carlsbad Caverns in New Mexico. Huong had read how a fifteen year old Mexican boy they called The Kid had been the only one brave enough to help a cowboy explore the Carlsbad Caverns way back in 1901. How proud Huong's parents would be if he discovered something important!

"I hope a big, old bear doesn't live in here," Darnell said with a nervous chuckle.

"I don't hear any growling," Huong said, sweeping the flashlight beam around the damp walls of the cave.

"Look how shiny the walls are,"

Darnell said. "Man, it's spooky in here!"

"It's like a tunnel leading to a bigger room," Huong said. "I bet we'll find a big room with stalagmites and stalactites!"

Outside the cave two figures moved stealthily. They had followed Huong and Darnell from school. Now they crawled up behind the huge boulder and using sticks for leverage they moved it. A small rumble turned into a roar as the rock tumbled down over the entrance to the cave.

"All right!" Josh yelled gleefully. "Now let's get outta here, Mick!"

"It'll take them 'till Christmas to get outta there," Mick laughed.

"What was that?" Darnell asked Huong.

"A big landslide, I think," Huong said, his eyes growing wide. "The big boulder! Maybe it fell!"

The boys made their way back to

the entrance they had just used. It was now blocked by the boulder.

"Oh, no!" Darnell gasped, "We're trapped!"

"But how did it happen?" Huong cried.

"Maybe those creeps from school followed us and pushed the boulder," Darnell said. "I thought I heard laughing, but I figured it had to be my imagination. Come on, let's both push and see if we can move it."

Huong and Darnell pushed with all their might, but they couldn't move the boulder half an inch.

"A lever," Huong said, "we would have to exert less force if we had a lever, some stick."

"Here's a stick," Darnell said.

The boys tried to use a small rock to hold the stick at a slant while they pushed the end of it under the boulder, but the stick quickly cracked.

For the first time since the boulder

rolled over the entrance to the cave, Huong felt fear. But he knew he couldn't give in to it. They had to find another way out of the cave. "Let's follow the tunnel," Huong said. "Maybe there's another entrance."

Darnell and Huong inched their way down the tunnel until they reached a tiny room. "Look! Light!" Darnell cried.

Huong looked up at the ceiling. "There's a crack up there. It looks like a big rock broke and made it."

"But it's not big enough for us to crawl through," Darnell groaned.

"Maybe I could crawl through," Huong said. "I am very slender and small. I haven't liked being that way before, but maybe now it's a good thing."

"Huong, you'd get stuck, and then what would I do?" Darnell said.

"No, I'm sure I can make it. Just boost me up, Darnell," Huong said.

"Okay, climb on my shoulders," Darnell said.

Huong climbed onto Darnell's broad shoulders and gained a toehold in the wall of the cave. He reached for the crack. With a mighty effort he tried to ease his body through the narrow chasm above. He was shaking with fear. What if Darnell was right and he got stuck?

Chapter 8

It was so narrow that Huong scraped his wrists and his thighs. Huong felt as if he were truly wedged in a granite pincer. But he pushed with all his strength. His parents had told him of the desperate boat trip they'd taken to reach freedom, how they suffered in refugee camps. But they made it to America. Huong had learned from them that you can do extraordinary things if you must.

"Push, Huong, push," Darnell yelled. "I'm praying for you. I'm praying, man."

Huong sucked in his breath to make himself skinnier and then pushed and the upper part of his body was free!

Now he needed only to pull his legs through. His arms were scraped and bleeding but a big smile danced on his face. "I made it, Darnell! Ohh, but it's snowing! It's a blizzard. I cannot make it back to the school. I must get help closer."

"Help from where?" Darnell shouted from inside the cave. He looked longingly up at the crack Huong had just escaped through. If only he could make it too, but he was much too big.

"Don't worry, Darnell," Huong shouted through the crack, "I will bring back help."

"You'll fall in a snowdrift and freeze to death," Darnell yelled.

"Have courage," Huong said, scrambling over the icy earth. He glanced over the white land to nearby Crow's Peak. Mr. Lattimore would surely come and help if he knew lives were at stake. He was Huong's only hope.

Huong headed for Crow's Peak, stumbling in deep drifts that almost buried his small body. He had never felt such cold in his life. If only Mr. Lattimore would come to the door and listen to his plea, then everything would be all right.

Huong struggled up the hill towards the man's log cabin. A little spiral of smoke escaped his chimney. Huong's teeth chattered with the cold. How wonderful to enter a warm place!

Huong's legs were numb when he reached the log fence around the cabin. He opened the rickety gate and moved slowly across the yard towards the door. As he did, the fierce barking of dogs exploded. Huong stopped in terror, thinking large, fierce dogs would tear him apart.

When Huong realized the dogs were not coming out, he raised a trembling hand and rapped on the door.

"Mr. Lattimore," Huong shouted

above the howling wind "please come out."

The door sprang open and the wild, harried man cried, "What are you doing on my property?"

"Mr. Lattimore, my friend is trapped by a boulder in the cave, and if we don't get him out I'm afraid he will freeze," Huong said.

The man stared at Huong for a few minutes, then he slammed the door. Huong almost broke into sobs of despair. He turned and stumbled away. Then he saw a shadow on the snow. Mr. Lattimore had come out, shovel in hand. His face was a mask Huong could not read.

Huong had to run to keep up with the man's long strides as they approached the cave.

"There, there's the rock," Huong said. "We could not move it."

Lattimore stood at the rock, stabbing the earth underneath it with his shovel.

Then, wordlessly, he went to find a long branch, making a lever. In just a few minutes the boulder rolled from its place and away from the cave entrance.

The snow was now falling so thickly that Huong could scarcely see in front of him.

Chapter 9

"This way," the man said sharply leading the way back towards his cabin. He marched at a fast pace with Darnell and Huong following him silently. When they reached his cabin he barked, "Inside with you!"

As the boys entered, two large wolf-like dogs, growling softly, watched them but did not move. A raccoon with a missing foot stared at the boys with curiosity from a perch on the wall. A big red cat sat in a box by the fire. A hawk with a broken wing peered from a cage.

"Fools, why are you out in this weather?" the man demanded.

Huong and Darnell looked at one

another. Huong found the courage to speak first. "We wanted to explore the cave. We thought there would be plenty of time before the snow came. But we think some bad boys pushed the boulder down to make trouble for us."

Lattimore went to the stove and put on a pot of water. "You are from that school where they call me wild man," he shoved his thick, gray mane of hair away. "They live in town and come into the wilderness. Their noisy, smelly cars and screeching radios tear up the land and disturb the peace. They kill the animals, start fires and landslides, and they call me wild!"

Huong looked closely at the man and saw a terrible sadness in his eyes. It was the sadness Huong often saw in his own father's eyes. Huong believed it came from a man witnessing terrible scenes of war's cruelty. Huong's father had been a lawyer in Vietnam, but the horrors of war scarred him so much. Now he was content to cook in a restaurant.

"I think you have been to Vietnam where so many of our people and your people died," Huong said. "I see sorrow in your eyes—the same sorrow that is in my father's eyes. I understand because he, too, is often angry at little things, and very sad and moody."

Lattimore served the two boys hot chocolate and then, when the blizzard passed, the sky was blue again, he flung open the door. "Go home now," he said. "And tell them in your school to stay away from me. Leave me with my wolves and my broken-winged hawk. Leave me in peace!"

"Let's go," Darnell said, grabbing Huong's arm.

Huong looked back at the man. His back was turned but his shoulders rocked as if he was crying. "We didn't even thank him," Huong remembered.

"Come on," Darnell said, "he'll probably change his mind and sic the dogs on us. Man, am I glad to get out of there."

"Poor, sad man," Huong said. "It's terrible how the kids at school make fun of him."

"Come on, Huong. If we don't run the snow will start again," Darnell yelled.

"Yes, you're right," Huong said, sprinting along beside Darnell.

When they reached the school, Josh and Mick were still doing chores for the janitor as part of their detention. Darnell stopped beside Josh and said, "You pushed the rock in front of the cave, didn't you?"

"Me? I don't know what you're talking about," Josh said with a silly grin.

The Janitor came around the corner then. "You boys ducked out of there for more than an hour this morning. Is that what you were doing—pushing boulders over cave entrances to make trouble for people?"

"Nah," Josh began, his face turning red and his mouth twitching.

"I think the principal just might want you boys on detention for the rest of the year," the janitor said, herding Josh and Mick before him.

Chapter 10

When Huong came home, he found his father tending to the stove. "I was worried about you, son," he said. "Such a bad storm came up."

"I'm fine, Father," Huong said. "Tell me, at the restaurant where you work, do they have cakes?"

"Cakes? Oh, yes. Very fancy cakes, son. Why do you ask?"

"I want to bring a cake to someone who has done me a great favor. Could the words 'thank you, my friend,' be put on the cake?" Huong asked.

"Oh, yes," Huong's father said.

"I have earned some money this fall raking leaves for some neighbors. Father, here is the money for a cake.

When you return home from work tomorrow morning, would you please bring me a cake," Huong asked.

"Very good. It is a good thing to show gratitude for favors done. This will serve you well in life, Huong," the older man said.

The next day dawned bright and clear and cold. Sunlight made the large banks of snow sparkle like precious jewels. It was a long walk to school, but Huong didn't mind it. He wore two sweaters, and he actually enjoyed all the beautiful scenes he passed along the way.

Huong carried the large chocolate cake with butter cream frosting in a plastic container. He wrote a note with it that said, *Thank you, Mr. Lattimore for your kindness in helping my friend and I out. Also, thank you for caring about the beautiful land, because it is from God and we must treasure it. Respectfully, Huong Ngo.*

It was a ten minute walk up to Mr. Lattimore's cabin, but it didn't seem so far. Huong was so excited to be doing this that he seemed to spring up the hill without effort.

When Huong rapped on the door, the man growled from inside, "What do you want? Go away."

"I must see you," Huong said.

Finally, the door opened. Huong walked past the startled man and put the cake on the rough table in the center of the room. "I forgot to thank you. This is my way of saying thank you, sir," Huong said.

Mr. Lattimore simply stared from the cake to the boy. He said nothing. Huong walked slowly towards the door. Huong was outside, a few feet away from the cabin when he heard the man sobbing. He was sitting in a chair, his back hunched over. Huong went back inside and put his hand gently on the man's back. "My father was a soldier, too. He often weeps. A soldier sees much sorrow and pain. The world doesn't understand. A soldier is hurt in ways the world cannot see. I'll go now. I won't bother you," Huong said.

The man suddenly looked up. "What did you say your name was?"

"Huong Ngo," Huong said. "I'm a freshman at Canyon Valley High School."

"I've lived here for ten years, and nobody has ever brought me a cake before," the man said.

Huong smiled. "I'm glad I did."

"Thank you, Huong. Come again," Mr. Lattimore said, the first smile anyone had seen on his face in over a dozen years breaking like a sunrise.

"I will," Huong promised. He hurried out across the snowy hills, feeling wonderful and strong and part of the nature that he, too, loved.